W9-AQR-213

Animal Time

Hide and Peek

Time to Read™ is an early reader program designed to guide children to literacy success regardless of age or grade level. The program's three levels correspond to stages of reading readiness, making book selection straightforward, and assuring that when it's time for a child to read, the right book is waiting.

Level 1
Beginning to Read
- Large, simple type
- Basic vocabulary
- Word repetition
- Strong illustration support

Level 2
Reading with Help
- Short sentences
- Engaging stories
- Simple dialogue
- Illustration support

Level 3
Reading Independently
- Longer sentences
- Harder words
- Short paragraphs
- Increased story complexity

For Won, with much love—LHH

For Dara and Walter—AW

Library of Congress Cataloging-in-Publication data
is on file with the publisher.

Text copyright © 2019 by Lori Haskins Houran
Illustrations copyright © 2019 by Albert Whitman & Company
Illustrated by Alex Willmore
First published in the United States of America
in 2019 by Albert Whitman & Company
ISBN 978-0-8075-7208-5

Printed in China
10 9 8 7 6 5 4 3 2 1 HH 24 23 22 21 20 19

Design by Morgan Beck

For more information about Albert Whitman & Company,
visit our website at www.albertwhitman.com.

100 Years of Albert Whitman & Company
Celebrate with us in 2019!

Animal Time

Hide and Peek

Lori Haskins Houran

illustrated by
Alex Willmore

Albert Whitman & Company
Chicago, Illinois

Bird heard a peep.

Peek, Bird!

It's just Ape.

Bird heard a peep.

Peek, Bird!

It's just Sloth.

Bird heard a peep.

Peek, Bird!
It's just—

EEEEEEK!

Bird heard a peep.

Peek? Please?

It's just Mouse.

Bird heard a peep.

Bird did not eek.
Bird did not peek.

It was just...

hide-and-seek!